This book belongs to:

_____

Digital art by Callaway Animation Studios under the direction of David Kirk
in collaboration with Nelvana Limited.

This book is based on the TV episode "Captain Sunny Patch," written by Michael Stokes, from the animated TV
series *Miss Spider's Sunny Patch Friends* on Nick Jr., a Nelvana Limited/Absolute Pictures Limited co-production in
association with Callaway Arts & Entertainment, based on the Miss Spider books by David Kirk.

Nicholas Callaway, President and Publisher
Cathy Ferrara, Managing Editor and Production Director
Toshiya Masuda, Art Director • Nelson Gomez, Director of Digital Services
Joya Rajadhyaksha, Associate Editor • Amy Cloud, Associate Editor
Bill Burg, Digital Artist • Keith McMenamy, Digital Artist • Christina Pagano, Digital Artist
Raphael Shea, Senior Designer • Krupa Jhaveri, Designer

Special thanks to the Nelvana staff, including Doug Murphy, Scott Dyer, Tracy Ewing, Pam Lehn,
Tonya Lindo, Mark Picard, Jane Sobol, Luis Lopez, Eric Pentz, and Georgina Robinson.

Library of Congress Cataloging-in-Publication Data available upon request.

Distributed in the United States by Penguin Young Readers Group.

Callaway Arts & Entertainment, its Callaway logotype,
and Callaway & Kirk Company LLC are trademarks.

ISBN 978-448-45012-4

Visit Callaway Arts & Entertainment at www.callaway.com.

10 9 8 7 6 5 4 3 2 1   08 09 10

Printed in China

Miss Spider's SUNNY PATCH FRIENDS

Captain Sunny Patch

David Kirk

CALLAWAY

NEW YORK

2008

"Sky Chiefs to the rescue!"

Squirt, Dragon, and Shimmer were playing superheroes. Dragon and Shimmer zipped through a dandelion patch at top speed.

"Wait!" Squirt complained. "I saw those first!"

"But we Sky Chiefs can fly!" shouted Shimmer as she and Dragon flew off.

Squirt scowled as he watched
them go. "If I'm going to be
a super-duper hero," he said,
"I have to figure out how to fly."

Squirt tried to use dandelion seeds and leaves for wings, but they didn't work.

He rushed to an abandoned hummingbird's nest in the Hollow Tree. "These feathers will do," he declared.

With the feathers strapped to his arms and an acorn helmet on his head, Squirt leapt from a branch of the Hollow Tree.

"AAHHHH!" he screamed, crashing through a berry bush. He came out splattered bright blue!

A gust of wind swept him over the Village Square.

"Is that a bird?" asked Mr. Mantis.

"Or a bee?" gasped Eunice Earwig.

"No," said Pillbug, "it's . . . Captain Sunny Patch!"

As Squirt tried to control his flight, he heard a voice call out, "Help!"

Snack the ladybug squirmed on her back, unable to flip over. Quick as a flash, Squirt picked her up and dropped her in the shade.

"Thanks, whoever you are," Snack sighed.

When Squirt cleaned up and arrived home, the Cozy Hole was buzzing.

"Captain Sunny Patch has the strength of ten army ants," said Shimmer.

"And super-cyclone speed," added Dragon. "I wonder who he is?"

"Hmmm," said Miss Spider.

The next morning, Squirt dressed in his superhero costume and zoomed off to find bugs in need.

He tried to help Eddy find his mother, only to realize that the little earwig wasn't lost.

Squirt saw Pillbug trying to grab a berry that was out of reach.

"Let me help you," he offered, shaking the bush. Soon the ground was covered with berries.

"But I only needed one!" said Pillbug.

"Being a superhero is super-hard," decided Squirt. "Maybe I should go back to being me."

He was taking off his costume when a snake slithered through the grass.

"Oh no, she's headed for the village!" Squirt cried.

A shadow fell across the Village Square. Everybuggy shrieked and ran for cover.

"Ssso many tasssty treatssss," hissed the snake, closing in on the bugs.

"Stop right there, Scaly!" a voice rang out.

Everybuggy looked up to see Squirt whooshing down on his wings.

"It's Captain Sunny Patch!" cried Pillbug.

"No," said Dragon. "It's . . . Squirt!"

Squirt flew circles around the snake. Trying to follow him, the slithering serpent got dizzier and dizzier. Finally, she slunk away.

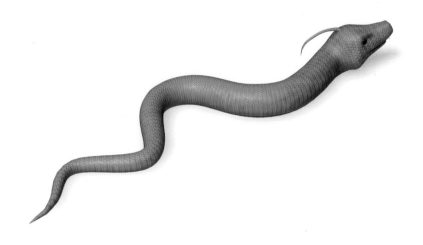

S quirt joined his family and friends.

"Wow!" said Dragon. "So *you're* Captain Sunny Patch?"

"Yeah," Squirt admitted, embarrassed, "but I still haven't learned how to land properly."

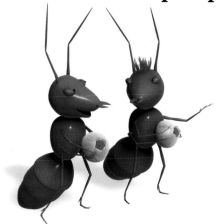

Miss Spider scooped Squirt up in her arms. "Captain Sunny Patch may not fly very well," she said, "but everybuggy who helps someone is a hero!"

Squirt grinned as everybuggy cheered.